For all my kitties, every day of the year:
Buckingham, Q, Aggie, Pippin, Kisses, Julie
(brrt), Curly + Percival, Hodge, and Po **–FF**

To my Dad, who always believed in my art and
who is dearly missed **–CL**

Library of Congress Cataloging-in-Publication Data available.

ISBN 978-1-4521-8461-6

Manufactured in China.

Text by Feather Flores.
Design by Lydia Ortiz and Angie Kang.
Typeset in Brothers and Recoleta.
The illustrations in this book were rendered in mixed media.

10 9 8 7 6 5 4 3 2 1

Chronicle Books LLC
680 Second Street
San Francisco, California 94107

Chronicle Books—we see things differently.
Become part of our community at
www.chroniclekids.com.

The Twelve Cats of Christmas

BY FEATHER FLORES   **ILLUSTRATED BY CARRIE LIAO**

chronicle books · san francisco

On the first day
of Christmas,
my true love gave to me

a kitten under the tree.

On the second day of Christmas,
my true love gave me *cats*:

TWO batting bows

and a kitten under the tree.

On the third day of Christmas,
my true love gave me *cats*:

THREE dressed up,

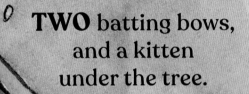

TWO batting bows,
and a kitten
under the tree.

On the fourth day of Christmas,
my true love gave me *cats*:

FOUR on the gifts,

THREE dressed up,
TWO batting bows,
and a kitten under the tree.

On the fifth day of Christmas,
my true love gave me *cats*:

FIVE purrs so sweet!

FOUR on the gifts,
THREE dressed up,
TWO batting bows,
and a kitten under the tree.

On the sixth day of Christmas,
my true love gave me *cats*:

SIX in the boxes,

FIVE purrs so sweet!
FOUR on the gifts,
THREE dressed up,
TWO batting bows,
and a kitten under the tree.

On the seventh day of Christmas,
my true love gave me *cats*:
SEVEN shredding paper,

SIX in the boxes,
FIVE purrs so sweet!
FOUR on the gifts,
THREE dressed up,
TWO batting bows,
and a kitten
under the tree.

On the eighth day of Christmas,
my true love gave me *cats*:

EIGHT watching winter,

SEVEN shredding paper,
SIX in the boxes,
FIVE purrs so sweet!
FOUR on the gifts,
THREE dressed up,
TWO batting bows,
and a kitten
under the tree.

On the ninth day of Christmas,
my true love gave me *cats*:

NINE chasing ribbons,

EIGHT watching winter,
SEVEN shredding paper,
SIX in the boxes,
FIVE purrs so sweet!

FOUR on the gifts,
THREE dressed up,
TWO batting bows,
and a kitten
under the tree.

On the tenth day of Christmas,
my true love gave me *cats*:

TEN helping Santa,

NINE chasing ribbons,
EIGHT watching winter,
SEVEN shredding paper,
SIX in the boxes,
***FIVE** purrs so sweet!*

FOUR on the gifts,
THREE dressed up,
TWO batting bows,
and a kitten
under the tree.

On the eleventh day of Christmas,
my true love gave me *cats*:

**ELEVEN
should be sleeping,**

TEN helping Santa,
NINE chasing ribbons,
EIGHT watching winter,
SEVEN shredding paper,
SIX in the boxes,
FIVE purrs so sweet!

FOUR on the gifts,
THREE dressed up,
TWO batting bows,
and a kitten under the tree.

On the twelfth day of Christmas,
my true love gave me *cats*:

**TWELVE cats
a-climbing,**

ELEVEN should be sleeping,
TEN helping Santa,

NINE chasing ribbons,
EIGHT watching winter,

SEVEN shredding paper,

SIX in the boxes,

FIVE *purrs so sweet!*

FOUR on the gifts,

THREE dressed up,

TWO batting bows,

and a kitten under the tree.

MEET THE
TWELVE CATS OF CHRISTMAS
and one kitten

Michael Cera "Mikey"

LIKES: Play fighting, ear scratches, stealing Maybe's sleeping spots

DISLIKES: Singing, bagpipes, Maybe's mess

FAVORITE CHRISTMAS ACTIVITY: Playing with long ribbons

Julius P. Mitten "Julie"

LIKES: Chin scratches, butter, being wrapped around his human's shoulders

DISLIKES: Surprises, getting bossed around, pens that he hasn't knocked off the table

FAVORITE CHRISTMAS ACTIVITY: Hiding in the branches of the tree

Maybe

LIKES: Broccoli, smacking bugs, rummaging in the cupboards

DISLIKES: Beestings, pedicures, Mikey's love bites

FAVORITE CHRISTMAS ACTIVITY: Eating the turkey dinner

Hodge

LIKES: Sunning in the kitchen window, batting around toy mice, snuggling his fuzzy wool blanket

DISLIKES: Dogs, not getting to eat his brother's food, being alone

FAVORITE CHRISTMAS ACTIVITY: Sniffing every single present

Bartholomew Boris "Bean"

LIKES: Raspberries, tortilla chips, doing tricks

DISLIKES: Not being the center of attention, going to the vet, the cat next door

FAVORITE CHRISTMAS ACTIVITY: Occupying empty stockings

Fluffy

LIKES: Belly scratches, peace and quiet, walking across computer keyboards

DISLIKES: Strangers, not getting enough treats, losing her toys under the couch

FAVORITE CHRISTMAS ACTIVITY: Claiming empty boxes once the gifts have been opened

Citra

LIKES: Sleeping on her humans, playing with leaves, head scratches

DISLIKES: The vacuum, houseguests, her own sneezes

FAVORITE CHRISTMAS ACTIVITY: Tearing up wrapping paper

Stella

LIKES: Bonito fish flakes, long pieces of string, drooling

DISLIKES: When the furniture gets rearranged, seeing the bottom of the food bowl, closed doors

FAVORITE CHRISTMAS ACTIVITY: Sleeping under the tree

Roo

LIKES: Chirping at birds, scratching the couch, sleeping on top of the fridge

DISLIKES: Loud noises, being woken up, not getting fed on time

FAVORITE CHRISTMAS ACTIVITY: Playing with crumpled wrapping paper

Eddy

LIKES: Playing fetch with paper airplanes, drinking milk from unattended cereal bowls, open windows

DISLIKES: Cat costumes, his scratching post, his tail

FAVORITE CHRISTMAS ACTIVITY: Attacking gifts as they're being wrapped

Faith

LIKES: Performing cat opera, munching leaves, yoga videos

DISLIKES: When breakfast is late, going for walks, not being allowed to lick the ice cream bowl

FAVORITE CHRISTMAS ACTIVITY: Wearing an elf collar

Ellie

LIKES: Eating houseplants, throwing up houseplants, chasing crickets

DISLIKES: Car rides, closed doors, her daily pill

FAVORITE CHRISTMAS ACTIVITY: Chewing on ornaments

Hosico

LIKES: Rubbing against people's legs, sleeping on his back, fitting into small spaces

DISLIKES: When his cat grass is too dry, being held, bath time

FAVORITE CHRISTMAS ACTIVITY: Watching his humans decorate the tree

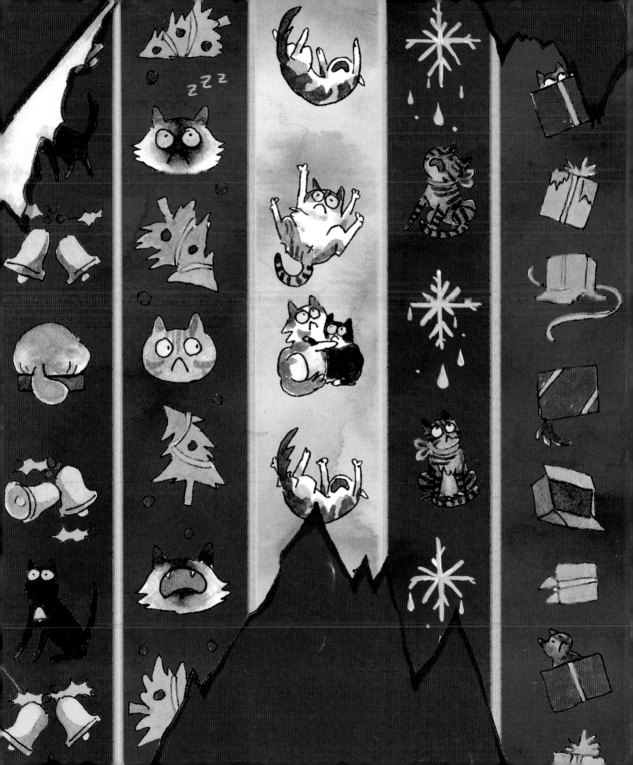